Elsie's Story
This Story Has No Hero

Written by: Michael Murphy

Illustrated by: Carissa McDonald

Kindle Direct Publishing

Copyright 2018 by Michael Murphy.

All rights reserved. No part of this book may be copied or reproduced electronically or by other means except for short quotes used in reviews without the express written consent of the author. The exception to this policy is the "Elsie's Story Character Test" which may be reproduced and copied for educational and classroom use.

MURLOR BOOKS

DEDICATION

For Lori

This book is also dedicated to the many students I have taught over the years, especially those at Risco R-2 Schools. It has been my life's honor and privilege to have been your teacher.

This is a work of fiction. Any resemblance to persons living or dead is purely coincidental.

Elsie's Story:
This Story Has No Hero

I want to set the record straight. I am not the hero of this story. This story has no hero.

It is a story that begins in a fourth grade classroom somewhere in Middle America. The **Heartland**. I won't tell you more about the location other than that. The location doesn't matter. It could have happened anywhere.

The story ends, nearly forty years later, in a middle school classroom.

A lot has happened in between.

My name is Timothy. I was a fourth grade student at Southlake Elementary School. I remember it being the biggest building I had ever seen. It was a two-story red brick structure divided into three main sections. First and second grades were housed in the east wing, third and fourth grades in the center section, and fifth and sixth grades in the west wing. Large windows dominated the outside of the building. The main entrance was in the center of the building and contained six large double doors. Most kids entered the school through those doors. It was **imposing** and very **institutional**. And, just a tad bit scary. I think most of the kids felt that way.

The building still exists but it's no longer a school. Today it is a nursing home. It's **ironic** that the same building that once served to educate young children now is the residence of many of those same kids living out their golden years.

I wasn't much different than any other kid in my class. We were typical kids. It was the early 1960's. Most of the upheavals that were to rock America- the **Civil Rights Movement, Vietnam,** and the **Counter-culture-** had not yet touched our small town. Living in Middle America like we did meant we were still stuck in the 1950's in a lot of ways. We were more concerned with Little League baseball and softball games and with what movies were playing at the Imperial Theater that week than with any social or political issues.

Most of all we were kids – and as you know – kids can be cruel.

That fourth grade year came back to me today. So I want to tell this story about that year. Like I said at the beginning – don't look for heroes. This story has no hero.

That year our class picked up a new student. We had a fairly large class for our small town. One hundred and seventy five kids divided into six different classrooms. That meant there were roughly thirty kids per

class. My group had twenty-nine students which was probably why the new

student was assigned to our class. Mrs. Lindale was our teacher.

She was an older teacher, close to retirement. She only stood a little over 5 feet tall. Her hair was white as snow. I remember that she was strict, but I also remember that she was a good teacher. A caring teacher.

Back to that *new* student. You see, she wasn't really *new*. She hadn't moved in from another state or another school district. No – she had been **retained**. That meant she had been held back a year. She had failed to achieve passing grades in her fourth grade studies in the previous year and now she had to repeat that year in school.

Retention is not something schools do much anymore. Instead they try to get the student the help they need to succeed. But, in the early sixties, **retention** in grade was common practice. This is what had happened to our *new* classmate. Unfortunately, being **retained** also carried a certain **stigma.** Students who were held back often became targets for **ridicule** by their classmates.

Her name was Elsie. She was a small, frail little girl. Even though she was a year older than the rest of us, she was one of the smallest members of the class. By her size, she should have fit right in with us. *"Fit right in with us."* That seems **ludicrous** now that I look at that statement on this page. Elsie didn't fit in. Not at all.

You see, Elsie came from a very poor family. That was obvious. Her clothes were a little shabby. Her dresses were often torn and ragged. They weren't always clean. Her hair was a mousey brown color and hung limp and lifeless to her shoulders. It too wasn't always clean. Neither was Elsie. Her face was sometimes dirty. Sometimes it seemed she hadn't bathe in days. It wasn't Elsie's fault. She was just a kid. Her family was poor.

Poverty is a cruel master and it is difficult to overcome. For Elsie and her family it was probably a daily struggle. I had heard adults say about people like Elsie's family – "*They just don't know any better.*"

"*They just don't know any better.*" Maybe that was true. Maybe it wasn't. Maybe it was just a way for us to justify our indifference. All I know is that Elsie paid a price for that *lack* of wisdom.

A few weeks into the school year a few of the boys in my class- some of them friends of mine – began to play a "*game*" during recess. If they touched Elsie or if she touched them – or if they handled anything she had touched- the boy would shout "Elsie germs!" He would then run to another boy and "pass the germs" on to him. The game often continued until Elsie was in tears. This cruel behavior quickly passed from our class to the entire 4th grade and then on to the 5th and 6th grade boys as well. The "game" was even played in the classroom where the "germs" were passed with a knowing look and a swift, silent swipe of one boy's hand to another out of the view of Mrs. Lindale.

Elsie did have a few friends. A trio of girls befriended her. But, they could do little to help her. They too were **ostracized**, mostly because they were poor like Elsie. They were never targets of the "germ game." That special torment was reserved just for Elsie. But, her friends were **marginalized** just as she was.

Many of the other girls in the school were indifferent toward Elsie and her friends. Some of the girls in the school even participated in the game.

As I think back on those days, I'm sure I played that game too. Elsie was a **convenient** target. She was easy to pick on. Like the title says – this story has no hero.

It was supposed to be a joke. A funny trick to play on Elsie. I don't think any of us ever thought about her feelings. I don't think the question *"How does this make her feel?"* ever crossed our minds. The "joke" was played every day. "Elsie germs" were always being passed.

How did she bear it? I can't imagine how tough it must have been to come to school every day and face that. But she did. There's your hero if you need one!

One day, late in the school year, Mrs. Lindale sent Elsie to the school

nurse. She had learned of our **bullying** behavior and had sent Elsie out of

the class so she could scold us. I remember she said that our behavior was

reprehensible. That we should be ashamed of the way we had treated her. She expected more of us and wanted this "game" to stop now! She reminded us of an important rule: *"Treat others as you would like to be treated."* I remember feeling guilty and embarrassed. Many of my classmates felt the same.

For a few weeks, our behavior did change. I'm not saying we treated Elsie any better or with any **kindness**. She was simply ignored. But, then we forget the scolding. The game started again. It would be a long time before it would end.

We got older. We moved on to the next higher grade. 5th grade. 6th grade. Then on to Junior High. Elsie went with us. But so did the game. "Elsie germs" made the trip across town to the Junior High School.

The Junior High building was two stories. 7th grade on the top floor- 8th grade on the lower floor. There were staircases on both ends of the building, always crowded with students rushing to class. We were thirteen or fourteen years old. With our **hormones** raging, we were mature in some ways, but still immature in so many others. We were **self-conscious** about our appearance and worried about every little thing. Did we fit in? Were we popular? Did this person like you or not? And in the middle of all that

anxiety, a cruel game that had started in elementary school- still being played.

Then one day something happened. I had an opportunity to right a wrong. To take one small step to treat Elsie like a person. In effect, to be the hero. But in the end, I failed.

It was a typical day. It was late fall. We had been in school for a couple of months. Still feeling our way around the new school, we were coming in from lunch, rushing up the stairs to get to math class. I was vaguely aware of Elsie a few feet in front of me. Several students separated us. Suddenly the bustling traffic came to a sudden stop. One of the boys ahead of me crashed into Elsie. He jumped back as if he had just touched a live electrical wire. He turned to another boy right behind him and shouted "Elsie germs!" and quickly wiped his hand on the boy's shoulder.

Elsie had turned to see who had crashed into her. I remember how **ashen** faced she seemed. How all alone on that crowded stairwell. How **crestfallen** to hear that taunt again.

The boy in front of me turned and repeated the phrase –"Elsie germs!"- and wiped his hand on my arm. Remember, I had played this game before. No hero here.

But something inside me said "No – not this time – not ever again."

I looked down at my arm, then back up at the two boys who stood expectantly in front of me. They were waiting for me to carry on the game, to pass on the germs. Instead I said: "Will you guys grow up? Leave her alone. What did she ever do to you?"

I don't remember if I looked at Elsie. If I did that memory is gone. The traffic on the stairs began to move. We went on to class. I don't know what Elsie thought or felt. I don't even know if she heard me.

I know what you're thinking. It sounds a bit like I had done something heroic. But I hadn't.

You see by that afternoon the **taunts** had started. "Timothy's got a girlfriend!" "Timothy loves Elsie!" Typical 7th grade stuff. Because of what I had said on the stairs, I had become a target. And that was not something you wanted to be in the 7th grade.

For the next few weeks I endured those taunts. But I survived. Soon the incident was forgotten. Things returned to normal for me.

However, for Elsie nothing changed. My words on the stairs that day had no effect. No one's behavior had been changed. I truly might have been the hero of this story if I had done more that day – and in the days that followed. What if I had befriended Elsie? What if I had done more to stop my classmates' behavior? What if I had done the right thing way back in the

4th grade? But I hadn't. **Ultimately,** I had failed one of the most basic tests of one's character. No hero here!

Elsie gradually drifted off my radar. I don't think I spoke more than fifty words to her over the next couple of years. Soon we were off to high school.

Elsie was soon gone too. When she was sixteen she became a **dropout**. Who could blame her?

And now it is nearly forty years later. It's sometimes strange what memories stay with us. That 4th grade year and that day on the staircase have stayed with me over the years. Occasionally, I find myself thinking about Elsie. It usually happens when I read about some unkind act or see someone mistreat another person. I wonder what happened to Elsie. I wonder how her life turned out. I wonder how our **bullying** behavior affected her.

Today was one of those days that Elsie came back to mind.

You see I'm a teacher now. I am standing in front of a classroom instead of sitting in the back of one. Many of my students remind me of me. They remind me of us.

I teach social studies to middle school students. Students the same age as I was that day on the staircase. I teach them history and government and geography. I try to make them aware of the world around them. My school also has a program designed to teach students about **character**. The

curriculum is called "Character Education." We try to teach our students

about **honesty**, and **responsibility**, and **accountability**. Today's lesson was about **kindness**. And in the middle of that lesson Elsie came back to me again.

The students were working through an assigned exercise on **kindness**. The exercise focused on how this character trait should be defined and asked students to list actions that could illustrate kindly behavior. Halfway through the lesson I stopped them. Instead of the assigned work, I told them Elsie's story.

I began by saying: "I am not the hero of this story. This story has no hero."

I hope I told it well. They seemed to be listening. They seemed to understand.

When the story was over I told them that I hoped that Elsie had found some peace in her life. That somewhere she was happy. But I was afraid that was not true. The hurt we experience when we are young can linger long in our memories and have lasting impact. I told them that I was afraid her life had been very complicated because of our actions.

As the class was nearing its end, I wanted to make another point. I explained that I was aware that from their point of view what had happened to Elsie had occurred a long time age. Our **bullying** of Elsie had been up-

close and very personal. Elsie knew exactly who her tormentors were.

I walked over and let my hand rest on the computer monitor that occupied a **prominent** place on my desk. Forty years ago, I stated, we didn't have the Internet. **Social media** didn't exist. **Cyber bullying** was unknown. Your generation has so many new opportunities to explore the world, to access information, and to make connections through these mediums. But the Internet and social media could also be very dangerous tools. I cautioned them about using the Internet to **denigrate** or belittle another classmate or person. Unlike our bullying of Elsie, **cyber bullying** could be impersonal and anonymous. Both types of **bullying** were equally cruel and destructive.

As the bell rang to end the period, I held the students for a moment to add one final plea. I told the students that I hoped that if they ever had an unkind thought –that if they were ever tempted to say something or do something that might hurt someone else- that they might think about Elsie. I also told them that I hoped that their **character** was stronger than mine. That if they saw someone being bullied or mistreated, they would step in and say something to stop such behavior. **"Kindness,"** I said "can not be

learned from a piece of paper. **Kindness** could only be learned from our actions – and from our mistakes."

Maybe Elsie's story will have an impact on them. Maybe it will give some meaning to the life Elsie's has led. Maybe they will remember her! I can only hope.

I must say this **refrain** once again: "This story has no hero."

But, maybe someday one of my students will change this ending.

And . . . if not one of them . . . maybe **YOU** can change the ending of this story!

"Knowing what's right doesn't mean much unless you do what's right."

--- Theodore Roosevelt

"Courage is fire, and bullying is smoke."

---Benjamin Disraeli

"We explain when someone is cruel or acts like a bully, you do not stoop to their level. Our motto is when they go low, you go high."

---Michelle Obama

"Freedom of Speech doesn't justify online bullying. Words have power, be careful how you use them."

---Germany Kent

"No one can make you feel inferior without your consent."

---Eleanor Roosevelt

"Friendship... is not something you learn in school. But if you haven't learned the meaning of friendship, you really haven't learned anything."

---Muhammad Ali

"I would rather be a little nobody, then to be an evil somebody."

---Abraham Lincoln

HONESTY

RESPECT

KINDNESS

COURAGE

integrity

FREINDSHIP

GENEROUS

GLOSSARY

accountability- the willingness to accept responsibility or to account for one's actions

anxiety – human emotion characterized by nervous behavior or unpleasant feelings of dread or doom

ashen- the pale gray color of ashes

bullying- to use superior strength or influence to intimidate someone or to torment that person

character- the good qualities of a person that usually include moral or emotional strength, honesty, and fairness

crestfallen- feeling shame or humiliation

curriculum- the course of study offered by an educational institution such as a high school or college

Civil Rights Movement- a movement to gain equal opportunity, social and economic justice, and voting rights for African-Americans and other minorities that took place in the 1950's and 1960's

convenient- involving little trouble or effort

Counter-culture- an attitude of some young people in the late 1960's and early 1970's that rejected the traditional values of their parents and promoted a different set of values and lifestyles; characterized by the term "hippie"

cyber bullying- the use of electronic communication to bully a person, typically by sending messages of an intimidating or threatening nature

denigrate- To attack the character or reputation of; speak ill of; defame. To disparage; belittle

dropout- someone who has left an educational institution without completing the course of instruction

Heartland- the central part of the United States; the Midwest

honesty- a character trait in which a person is fair and truthful in his or her dealings with other people

hormones- chemical messengers that are secreted directly into the bloodstream which help the organs and tissues carry out their functions such as growth and development

imposing- grand and impressive in appearance

institutional- a characteristic of an established organization that has an important role in the life of a nation such as a church, government, school, or bank; sometimes characterized as uniform, dull, or unimaginative

ironic-coincidental; unexpected; happening in the opposite way to what is expected, and typically causing amusement because of this

kindness- a personal quality of being friendly, considerate, and generous

ludicrous- so foolish, unreasonable, or out of place to be amusing or ridiculous

marginalized- to discriminate against or treat a person as if they are insignificant

ostracized- exclude someone from a society or group of people

poverty- the state of being very poor; having a lack of goods and services commonly taken for granted by most members of a society

prominent- standing out or projecting beyond a surface or line; readily noticeable

refrain- a repeated line or number of lines in a poem, song, or story; a comment that is repeated

reprehensible- open to criticism or rebuke; blameworthy

responsibility- worthy of another person's trust or confidence; reliable and dependable

retained- the act of requiring a student to repeat a class or a year of school because of insufficient academic progress

retention- a school policy requiring students to repeat classes or a school year for failure to maintain acceptable academic standards

ridicule- to deride or make fun of

self-conscious- feelings of undue awareness of oneself, one's appearance, or one's actions

social media- websites and other online means of communication that are used by large groups of people to share information and to develop social and professional contacts

stigma- a mark of disgrace or infamy; a stain or reproach, as on one's reputation

taunt- to provoke or challenge someone with insulting remarks

ultimately- finally; in the end; at the most basic level

Vietnam- a country in Southeast Asia that was the site of a decade long war between the United States and its ally South Vietnam and communist forces led by North Vietnam. The war deeply divided Americans; those who supported the war were called 'hawks' and those opposed to it were called "doves.' The war ended in 1975 with the collapse of South Vietnam.

SOURCES

The definitions listed above are credited to the websites listed below:

Dictionary.com. Available @ https://www.dictionary.com

Merriam-Webster. Available @ https://www.merriam-webster.com

Oxford Dictionaries. Oxford University Press. Available @ https://www.oxforddictionaries.com

The Free Dictionary. Available @ https://thefreedictionary.com

"Elsie's Story Character Test"

Name_____**Class**_____**Date**_____

Part 1: Matching Terms: Match the term from the list with the correct definition below. Write the correct letter in the space provided.

TERMS:

A. crestfallen   G. anxiety
B. taunt   H. bullying
C. kindness   I. imposing
D. retained   J. accountability
E. honesty   K. stigma
F. character   L. responsibility

_____1. a character trait in which a person is fair and truthful in his or her dealings with other people

_____2. worthy of another person's trust or confidence; reliable and dependable

_____3. feeling shame or humiliation

_____4. human emotion characterized by nervous behavior or unpleasant feelings of dread or doom

_____5. the act of requiring a student to repeat a class or a year of school because of insufficient academic progress

_____6. grand and impressive in appearance

_____7. to provoke or challenge someone with insulting remarks

_____8. the willingness to accept responsibility or to account for one's actions

_____9. the good qualities of a person that usually include moral or emotional strength, honesty, and fairness

_____10. a mark of disgrace or infamy; a stain or reproach, as on one's reputation

_____11. a personal quality of being friendly, considerate, and generous

_____12. to use superior strength or influence to intimidate someone or to torment that person

Part Two: Thought Questions: Provide a brief explanation for each question below.

1. What characteristics did Elsie possess that made her a target for the bullying behavior of her classmates?

2. After the incident in the 7th grade stairwell, why do you think the character of Timothy failed to befriend Elsie? Do you think he was a target of bullying also? Why?

3. Mrs. Lindale attempted to change the students' behavior toward Elsie. Why do you think her effort did not have a long-lasting impact on Elsie's classmates?

4. Most of the bullying behavior directed toward Elsie came from the boys in her class. The story states that many of the girls in the class were participants in the "germ game" or were indifferent toward Elsie. Why do you think more of the girls failed to stand up for Elsie?

5. You may have heard the statement that someone "has cooties." Do you think the "germ game" was similar to this type of statement? Are both statements a form of bullying behavior?

6. At the end of the story Timothy states that he hopes his students will "change this ending." What do you think he means by this statement?

7. Social media is often used to bully and intimidate people. Do you think people who abuse these forms of communication should be banned from their use? Why or why not?

Part Three: Multiple Choice: Read each question carefully and select the best answer to each question by writing the letter in the space provided.

_____1. What class is Timothy teaching near the end of the story when he recalls his memories of Elsie and then relates her story to his students?

   A. Geography   B. Character Education   C. History   D. Government

_____2. The story follows Elsie into high school. What happens to her after she enters high school?

   A. she becomes an honor student   B. she transfers to another school
   C. she confronts those who bullied her   D. she becomes a dropout

_____3. Which key word used in the story means open to criticism or rebuke; blameworthy?

   A. reprehensible   B. ludicrous   C. convenient   D. ostracized

_____4. In what elementary grade does the cruel game of passing "Elsie's germs" begin?

   A. 5th B. 6th C. 4th D. 7th

_____5. Timothy, the story teller, relates that Southlake Elementary School is no longer a school today. What is it instead?

   A. a nursing home   B. a government office
   C. an apartment complex   D. an abandoned building

_____6. Elsie was older than her classmates. How much older was she?

   A. two years   B. one year   C. just a few months   D. three years

_____7. Which key word used in the story means so foolish, unreasonable, or out of place to be amusing or ridiculous?

   A. marginalized   B. ostracized   C. convenient   D. ludicrous

_____8. In the story when the incident takes place in the 7th grade stairwell, to which class are the students going to when they are rushing up the stairs?

   A. Social Studies   B. Science   C. Math   D. English

_____9. Which key word used in the story means feelings of undue awareness of oneself, one's appearance, or one's actions?

   A. refrain   B. institutional   C. ashen   D. self-conscious

_____10. The author repeats the line "this story has no hero" throughout the story. This is an example of the use of a _____?

   A. metaphor   B. simile   C. refrain   D. taunt

Part Four: Completion: Use the words from the "Word Bank" to complete each statement below.

WORD BANK:

Cyber bullying	ashen	hormones
retention	curriculum	Civil Rights Movement
institutional	poverty	ostracized
Counter-Culture	Heartland	convenient

1. To be _____ is to exclude someone from a society or group of people.

2. The word _____ is defined as a characteristic of an established organization that has an important role in the life of a nation such as a church government, school, or bank; sometimes characterized as uniform, dull, or unimaginative.

3. _____ is the use of electronic communication to bully a person, typically by sending messages of an intimidating or threatening nature

4. A _____ is the course of study offered by an educational institution such as a high school or college

5. The _____ was an attitude of some young people in the late 1960's and early 1970's that rejected the traditional values of their parents and promoted a different set of values and lifestyles; characterized by the term "hippie."

6. _____ is defined as the pale gray color of ashes.

7. _____ is a term defined as involving little trouble or effort.

8. The _____ is the central part of the United States; the Midwest.

9. _____ is a school policy requiring students to repeat classes or a school year for failure to maintain acceptable academic standards.

10. _____ are chemical messengers that are secreted directly into the bloodstream which help the organs and tissues carry out their functions such as growth and development.

11. _____ is the state of being very poor; having a lack of goods and services commonly taken for granted by most members of a society.

12. The _____ was an effort to gain equal opportunity, social and economic justice, and voting rights for African-Americans and other minorities that took place in the 1950's and 1960's

Part Five: Short Essay: Compare and contrast the type of bullying that Elsie faced 40 years ago with the use of cyber bullying through the Internet and Social Media today. Is either more harmful or cruel than the other? What methods should be used to stop bullying in all its forms?

About the Author: Michael Murphy is a retired educator from Missouri who taught for over twenty-five years in Missouri's public schools and colleges. He holds a Bachelor of Arts degree from Murray State University and a Master's from the University of Mississippi. His work has been published in *Instructor, Poet Forum,* and the *Annual Conference of the Missouri National Guard Association.*

About the Illustrator: Carissa McDonald is a photographer, artist, and illustrator who currently lives in Sikeston, Missouri. She holds a Bachelor's degree in Photography from Southeast Missouri State University. Her photographic and artistic portfolio may be viewed at carissamcd.wixsite.com/photography.

Made in the USA
Monee, IL
13 February 2022

90426629R00026